Table of Contents

I0547930

A Tale of Two Threesomes, or How Gender is Irrelevant in D/s

by Ronda DeMure

Chapter One: Submissive

J im arrived at the restaurant first and sat at a table overlooking the front entrance. He had agreed to this breakfast meeting out of curiosity. According to her profile, Jill was not a submissive, so what interest could this woman have in him?

He smiled and rose to his feet to greet the well-dressed businesswoman when she came in a few minutes later. She was tall, only a couple of inches shorter than he was. Her 5'8" height, shoulder length blonde hair, and petite frame, combined with a professional demeanor, made a striking impression.

After ordering food and engaging in cursory small talk, Jim got right to the subject at hand. "Have you always been a domme, Jill?" He asked

"I've felt that way pretty much all of my life," Jill responded. "Although it wasn't until college that I began to act on it. That's when I started to dominate men. Actually, domination is the only way I've had relationships with men."

"Which causes me to wonder why you wanted to meet with me?" He cocked his head to the right. "Our interests clearly don't match up."

"Indeed!" Jill smiled, took a long slip of coffee, and then slowly put the mug back on the table. "The reason I wanted to meet with you, Jim," she answered slowly, "is that I was rather curious about the article you wrote about erotic spankings."

"Ah, you'd like to learn more about my technique?"

"In a way. Although, since my subs are men, I doubt that your technique would apply." She looked thoughtful. "But it made me think about what it might be like to experience a spanking, in the way in which you described it, for myself."

"Oh? Do you think that you could be curious about exploring a submissive side in yourself?"

"Possibly." She looked quizzical. "I never really thought I was, but recently I've been starting to think I might be oriented a bit that way."

"Maybe you're developing into a switch?"

"That might be true." She smiled again. "Seeing how my submissives become so aroused when I spank them has been causing me to be curious about being spanked myself. What it might be that they feel." She looked directly at Jim. She was pleased that he was taller than her; his height combined with salt and pepper hair caused him to carry an air of authority. "After reading your article about erotic spanking," she continued. "I went ahead and checked your profile. Your on line name is 'The Schoolmaster' and you describe yourself as a dominant who enjoys spanking?"

"That's correct."

"I'm curious. How did you come up with that moniker?"

"While I very much enjoy giving a good spanking, I also enjoy seeing women in short skirts. Particularly, a schoolgirl uniform. You'd probably call that a fetish of mine." He shrugged. "So taking both into consideration, calling myself the schoolmaster seemed logical."

"Ah, I see. You're a fan of the pleated skirt and white cotton panties look, eh?" Jill grinned.

"Indeed." He nodded affirmatively. "It makes for a great role play by instantly establishing the roles of authority figure and subordinate. So I look for women to spank who have a similar kink."

"Jim," Jill said as she stared into her coffee cup, formulating her question before looking back up at him. "I'd like to ask you to spank me?" Then, watching his facial response, quickly added, "But not in a dominant/submissive way. I don't want to have to do, err, anything."

"Or have me make you..." Jim voice tapered off as he smiled back at her expression.

"Right." She shook her head. "I don't want to do oral afterwards."

"Don't you make your subs thank you after a spanking?"

"Of course. As I'm sure you enjoy having yours on their knees after you're done as well." She bit her lower lip. "But, like I said, I really don't know if I do have a submissive orientation. I'll admit to being curious about being spanked, but that's the extent of it. What I do know is that I don't want to do oral."

"So, you're asking me for a one-time favor, just to satisfy your curiosity?"

"One dominant to another. Yes. Might you consider it as, say, a professional courtesy?"

"Hmm." Jim rubbed his chin thoughtfully.

"It's okay if you want to fuck me afterwards." Jill added quickly. "I know that after giving a spanking you're going to be turned on and in need of release. Actually," She smirked. "I'd like that too. As a dominant, I can't have a sub penetrate me. It's been a while since I had a cock instead of a tongue in my pussy."

"Perhaps." Jim nodded slowly and broke into a smile. "Provided you present yourself properly. Do you have a schoolgirl uniform?"

"As a matter-of-fact, I do." She chuckled. "I went to Catholic school and I'm sure that my old uniform is still somewhere in my closet. Although I haven't seen it in years."

"Very well, then. If you'll dress up for me, then I'll give you the erotic spanking you're asking for."

Jill beamed enthusiastically. "Thank you, Jim. Um, would you like to come to my house? We could meet there this Saturday afternoon?"

"That sounds splendid."

"Wonderful." Jill drained her coffee and rose to her feet. "I'd better get off to work now, but I look forward to seeing you on Saturday."

"Likewise." Jim remained seated and watched Jill as she walked away. It was going to be wonderful having this smartly dressed businesswoman converted into a schoolgirl.

Jim rang Jill's doorbell at 2 the following afternoon. The front door opened, but Jill hid herself behind it until Jim was inside. "I don't want any neighbors to see me dressed like this," she explained.

"No problem." Jim responded understandingly. "Not quite what they would expect of you, eh?"

"You can say that again." She giggled.

"I like your outfit, though," he said as he followed her into the living room.

"I'm afraid I've become a little broader in the beam than I was back in school, so the skirt is quite a bit shorter on me now. Do my panties show from behind?"

"Not that I can tell from here." Jim sat on the couch and beckoned to her. "But perhaps while I'm sitting down."

Jill stood in front of him and did a quick twirl, causing her skirt to playfully fly up and flash her white cotton panties. "How's that?" She giggled.

"That's nice, Jill." Jim leaned forward, raised the front hem of her skirt, told her to keep still, and unabashedly stared at her panties. They were bikini cut, wonderfully accentuating her long legs. "Very nice indeed."

Jill blushed, unsure of whether the compliment was about her panties or the fact she had no objections to what he was doing."

"Not quite regulation schoolgirl briefs, though." He looked up into her eyes. "Are they?"

"No sir." Jill licked her lips. "I thought you might prefer this style."

"You like it when I look up your skirt, don't you?" He asked, returning his gaze to her milky thighs.

"Umm, yes," she responded shyly. "Yes, I do."

Jim continued to hold her skirt up but again looked into her face. "Why do you think that is?"

"I don't know why, but it's incredibly erotic just standing here while you do." She bit her lower lip and her eyes widened while Jim's eyes returned to her panties. "I think, maybe, because it makes me feel vulnerable."

"And that is a big reveal into your submissive side. It is erotic, not because you are showing your panties, but the fact that you are being compliant by lifting your skirt on command. The fact you are excited by feeling vulnerable really underscores that." Jim released Jill's skirt. "And now, I trust that you're ready for your spanking?"

"Yes, Sir." She was almost trembling.

Jim pulled Jill face down across his lap. "Now I can see your panties from behind," he teased.

Jill immediately felt more relaxed, her arms dangling with her fingertips almost touching the floor, while Jim laid her skirt across her back and massaged her bottom through her panties. The rubbing soon gave way to light taps, then slaps, and as her bottom began to warm Jill started to squirm. "I see that keeping still may be an issue for you," he told her as he placed his left hand on the back of her neck. "But not at all insurmountable."

Four well places slaps later, Jim's right hand slid inside her panties and caressed her warm bottom. Her breathing became audible as he then eased her panties down to her knees before proceeding with a bare-bottomed spanking until he could hear her panting. "You're warming up nicely," he told her, firming his grip on her neck to hold her still while simultaneously engaging his right hand in a staccato of slaps until he suddenly stopped and slid his hand between her thighs. Her pussy was drenched. He massaged her engorged clitoris with his index finger for a few seconds, then withdrew his soaked hand and applied her juices across her glowing buttocks. "This both soothes," he told her. "And stings," he added as he applied a squarely placed slap.

Now audibly excited, Jill bucked without success against Jim's firm grip as he delivered the next series of spanks, but her writing was sufficient to cause her panties to slide past down to her ankles. She kicked them off.

"Now you're going to receive six of the best," Jim announced. He counted them out each time his hand made firm contact.

After the final, hardest slap, he plunged his thumb inside her, directly onto her g-spot, while his fingers alighted on her clitoris.

Jill's orgasm was almost instantaneous as soon as he squeezed his hand together.

Jim kept his fingers in place until Jill's twitching subsided, then slid her face down, onto the couch cushion next to him.

She remained bent over onto the couch with her knees on the floor while Jim stood up. He reached down and raised her skirt up over her back, enjoying the view of her glowing red bottom as he unfastened his trousers. His pants quickly discarded, he knelt on the floor behind her and teased her soaked vagina with the tip of his rigidity. She wriggled back and forth in an attempt to drive it inside, but he took control by holding onto her hips while he continued to tease her. Then, with a single, sudden thrust, he pushed himself deep inside. Jill's initial gasp quickly turned to moans as Jim began to rhythmically push back and forth. He then remained still and controlled the action by using his hands to slide her up and down his cock. Jill's second orgasm was concurrent with his subsequent explosive ejaculation inside her.

Jill remained leaning across the couch cushion as Jim eased away. He then assisted her to her feet and permitted her to put her panties back on, ogling her as she did so.

"That was fantastic," Jill beamed as she turned to face him. "A glass of wine?"

"Perfect." Jim sat back on the couch and Jill produced a tray with two glasses, a bottle of wine, and a corkscrew, which she placed on the coffee table in front of him. Jim opened the wine, and she sat on the couch next to him.

"Here's to your spanking," Jim toasted and quaffed a gulp.

Jill's eyes smiled at him as she sipped her wine.

"So, tell me," he inquired. "Was it as you had imagined?"

"It was absolutely incredible," Jill blurted enthusiastically, then drained her entire glass. "I suspected I might like being spanked, but now I'm sure."

"So, perhaps you've discovered that you do like erotic pain. Yes?"

"Oh, yes. The flow of pain into the pleasure of...well...it was unbelievably hot."

"Could this have provided your answer as to whether you have a submissive side?"

"Perhaps," she answered coyly. "I must admit that you do provide a wonderful spanking." She smirked. "And you had me cum twice, too."

"Always happy to oblige." Jim smiled at her.

"Really?"

"Indeed."

"Well, you know that I'm going to want to do that again, don't you."

"And you well know my requirement of you for doing so."

"You mean oral?"

"Precisely." Jim took a gulp of wine. "You expect your subs to service you orally, don't you?"

"Yes. But I just want to be spanked."

"As a submissive?"

"Mmm. It is beginning to look that way, isn't it?" Her mouth twisted. "But you got your release by fucking me and we can always do that again. Can't my pussy be enough for you?"

"It's very nice, Jill. And I'd be delighted to partake of it again." He smiled. "But I want the submissiveness of you thanking me. So, if you'd like another spanking, you'd have to do it as a sub, and that means you'd have to suck me." He looked thoughtfully at her. "Maybe I'd fuck you first, and then have you take it in your mouth."

"I really don't think I want to do that." Jill shook her head.

"That's unfortunate. I'd enjoy spanking you as a sub." He shrugged. His matter of fact demeanor reinforced the possibility that he was not going to make an exception for her.

The subject apparently closed, there was no more discussion about submission or spanking. Jim and Jill continued with pleasant conversation until the wine was finished and Jim announced that it was time for him to go.

"Thank you," Jill told him as she opened the front door for him to leave, once again hiding behind it.

"Still shy, eh?"

"Only to the outside world." She joined Jim in his chuckling. "But not for you."

"Thank you for the wine, Jill," he said as he left. "This has been a delightful afternoon." He turned, cocked his head to the right, and added, "And be sure to let me know if your desire for being spanked again overrides your resistance to doing something that you don't want to do."

Jill was unable to control her involuntary smirk as she closed the door.

Chapter Two: Allan

Two days later it was Jill providing the discipline with Allan, her long time submissive. Since Allan was only 5'6" and had a slender body, it had been very easy for Jill to establish the dominant/submissive roles for them almost from the first time they met. For today's session she was wearing a black leather bustier and a short, black leather skirt, the perfect combination of sexiness and dominance. She sat in a leather armchair while Allan stood attentively in front of her, head bowed and hands clasped behind his back. "I understand that you have been a naughty boy," she said in a monotone.

"Yes, mistress."

"Tell me."

"I masturbated without asking your permission, mistress."

"I see." Jill picked up a flogger from beside the chair with her right hand and tapped it into her left. "Then you are to be punished for doing so." She stood up and moved behind him, brandishing the flogger, and barked out a single-word order, "Strip!" Then, as Allan pulled his polo shirt up over his head, she swatted his upper back, adding, "Faster."

Allan was soon naked, and he remained compliantly standing while Jill attached a pink leather collar around his neck, clipped a matching leash to it, and led him to the chair that she had been sitting on. At her instruction of, "Bend over," he leaned forward and placed both hands on the cushion.

Jill began by flogging his buttocks, thighs, and upper back until his skin had been reddened to her satisfaction, then pushed the handle of the flogger sideways into his mouth. "Hold this," she told him. "Do not drop it." Then, positioning herself at his left side, she brought her right hand down onto his left bottom cheek with an audible slap. The next stroke went to the other side, following which she proceeded to randomly spank his buttocks until they were exhibiting an even, red glow. Her right hand tingling, she stopped and said, "Stand up," while she simultaneously pulled up on the leash. She removed the flogger from Allan's mouth and sat in the chair, teasing his ready-to-burst erection with the leather tip.

"Please, mistress." Allen begged in an almost whimper. "Please may I touch myself?"

"Soon," she replied as she again stood up and pulled down on the leash. "Provided you're a good boy." She pulled her skirt up to her waist as he knelt in front of her and slid her black lace panties off. Then, sitting back down on the chair, she spread her legs to present her pussy, peeking through light blonde curls. "You want to be a good boy, don't you?"

"Yes, please, mistress."

Jill gave Allen her panties and he obediently leaned forward to lick her while his right hand slid the panties over his already pulsing cock.

"Work your tongue," Jill ordered as she grabbed the two metal rings on each side of the collar and forced Allan's mouth hard against her. It was clear that he had already ejaculated, so now all of his attention was to dutifully bring her to orgasm with his tongue.

Allan complied, and Jill dug her hands into his hair as he brought her to completion. But the intensity she once felt was no longer there, and her mind flashed back to the orgasm that Jim had given her via his spanking days earlier. It far exceeded those she ever achieved as a dominant, and it occurred to her that she was harboring an intense craving to be spanked again. Perhaps even dominated. She needed to talk these feelings out, and since Allan was also a friend, she decided to confide in him. So, after he had dressed again and they were enjoying a post play drink, she broached the subject with him. "Allan," she began, a little nervously. "Can I ask you something rather personal?"

"Of course." Allan chuckled. "Considering our relationship, I can't imagine that there's anything that we can't ask each other."

"Well. I've recently become suspicious that I might also have a submissive side."

"That's wonderful to hear, Jill. The pleasure that being submissive provides is indescribable." He suddenly looked concerned. "You're not going to ask me to spank you or anything? I'm definitely sub, and couldn't possibly..."

Jill raised her right hand to quiet him. "No. Not at all," she laughed. "The fact is, I was recently spanked by a proper dominant. And, well. I liked it a lot."

"Well, of course you did. I frankly don't know what you get of being the spanker when being on the receiving end is so damn wonderful."

"It was." Jill was suddenly relaxed and opened up. "It was so intense that it made me quiver all over and brought me to tears, but it also gave me the most incredible orgasm." She bit her lower lip. "I never realized that I could be so turned on like that."

"Did he really spank you that hard?" Allan was intrigued.

"Oh Yes. Much harder than I ever could spank anyone."

"Mmm. I'd like a hard spanking too." Allan looked a little sheepish. "Do you think you might ask him if he'd spank me?" He asked tentatively.

"I doubt it. You're not a girl." Jill said, initially taking Allan's question as jest, but then realized from his expression that he might be serious. "Jim has a schoolgirl fetish," she added by means of explanation.

"I've often fantasized about being treated as a sissy. Do you think, if I dressed up...?"

"That I could talk to him about it?" Jill finished Allan's obvious thought. She knew from their scenes that Allan was turned on by humiliation and that he also liked wearing women's clothing. But this side of him had never occurred to her.

"Yeah," he said excitedly. "Would you do that for me?"

"I'll ask Jim and let you know what he says. But I wouldn't get your hopes up."

"Perhaps you could do something to sweeten the deal for him?" Allan gave her a sideways smile. "I'd really be appreciative."

"Well, all right," Jill slowly nodded affirmatively. "I'll see what I can do for you."

The thought of watching Jim spank Allan had caused a sudden arousal between Jill's legs. It was a thought that became an obsession for her as the day wore on. Part of her excitement in dominating Allan was the fact she humiliated him, and dressing him up as a schoolgirl and having him spanked by Jim was the most erotic humiliation imaginable. She determined to do her best to bring it about.

Knowing that Jim would most likely say no to spanking a man, rather than simply ask him, she would have to carefully bring it up in conversation. The best way to introduce the idea would be after a session, when they were both relaxed and he might be open to new ideas. In order for that to come about, though, she was first going to have to reconnect with him. And that would entail being submissive in the way he wanted.

She grinned to herself at that thought and the subsequent realization that what she had, just two days ago, insisted she did not want to do, had since become a desire. She already knew that Jim had the ability to give her spectacular orgasms. The surprise for her was her developing willingness to please him in return. And if Jim would humiliate sissy Allan for her, who knows what else she might be willing to do? She broke into a wide grin and sent a text to Jim. "I think I might be submissive. Can we talk?"

"Certainly. Let's meet for coffee," was his immediate response.

Jill arrived at the coffee shop first and had two mugs of coffee and a plate of pastries on the table when Jim arrived. She smiled while watching him take off his suit jacket and hang it over the back of the chair before sitting down. "Thank you for meeting with me," she said.

"It's my pleasure," Jim replied. "I'm so pleased that you're interested in exploring your submissive side."

"My spanking gave me so much to think about. And, the more I thought about it, the more I realized I was willing to do what you want in order to have you spank me again." She smirked. "Will I have to swallow?"

"Not necessarily." Jim smiled and looked at her over the top of his coffee mug. "You have a very attractive bottom."

"Oh no." Jill said as she vibrated her head from side to side, then broke into a wry smile. "I'll be fine with swallowing." She slid her lower teeth across her top lip. "But you'll have to make me do it. You know, force me."

"I like that." Jim nodded. "Do you also want me to order you to do things?"

"I think so." She wrapped her hands around her mug thoughtfully. "I've always felt that obedience is integral to submissiveness."

"Indeed it is." Jim reached for a pastry. "And how do you feel about bondage?"

"I have restraints at my house." She picked up a bear claw. "They make it easy for subs." She took a bite out of the pastry. "To do the things they want done to them." She smiled. "I have been a dominant for some time, you know," she explained.

"So you're seeing yourself as both domme and sub, then?"

"Possibly." She looked quizzical. "But I do need to delve more into the sub side first in order to find out." She looked up at Jim. "Will Saturday, at my house, work for you?"

"That will be perfect."

Chapter 3: Good Girl

J im made his way to Jill's house on Saturday morning and arrived precisely at 10 am. Jill, once again dressed in her schoolgirl uniform, greeted him warmly as soon as she had closed the front door. They then went into the kitchen where she proceeded to make coffee.

"Since we're going to be enjoying a D/s scene," Jim began. "We should talk about limits. Do you have any hard ones?"

She responded immediately with, "Just anal," remembering his coffee shop implication earlier.

"Have you ever tried?" He smiled. "There is one woman I know who really likes it." Lynn, Jim's submissive, had over the years actually developed a preference for being taken anally.

"No." Jill said tersely as she handed him a mug of coffee and sat at the table.

"It brings her to orgasm," he teased.

"I don't even want to try."

"No problem." Jim laughed and took a gulp of coffee.

"It's humiliating," she said, for some reason feeling the need to explain. "I sometimes use butt plugs on my subs, but they want to be humiliated."

"I understand," he said calmly. "Like I said, no problem."

"But, you like to do it?"

"Indeed! It is a perfect form of domination, you know."

Jill smiled at him. She thought his answer was a little cryptic, but didn't want to belabor the point. She was anxious for her spanking to commence. "Would you like more coffee?"

"No thanks." He smiled back. "I think you're looking quite ready for something else."

They drained their coffee mugs and proceeded into the living room. Jim stood behind her, put his hands on her shoulders, and whispered, "You're now going to do as you are told," into her left ear. "Do you understand?"

"Yes, sir."

"Splendid." He took her by the hand and led her to the couch where he sat, and then positioned her standing in front of him. "Lift up your skirt."

Jill raised the front of her skirt and kept still while Jim reached forward and stroked the front of her white cotton panties.

"Do you like showing your panties?"

"I like showing them to you, sir."

"I'm pleased," he said as he gently slid her panties down her long, slender legs. She obediently raised each foot as he tapped her ankles, and then tossed the panties onto the coffee table. He slid two fingers into the moist furrow beneath her blonde curls. "I see that it excites you." He leaned back. "And you're going to be a good girl for me?" He asked as he unfastened his silk tie."

"I'll be a good girl for you, sir." The trembling in her hands and increased breathing underscored Jill's growing excitement.

"Splendid." Jim rose to his feet as he slid his tie off. He tied one end of it around her right wrist. "You can let go of your skirt now," he told her has he pulled her wrists together and tied them behind her back. Her hands, now bound together, were pressed against the bulge in his pants as he stood close behind her. He slowly unbuttoned her blouse, then cupped each of her 32 B breasts and toyed with her nipples. "Tell me." he whispered into her right ear. "What to good girls do?"

"Good girls suck cock." The excitement of saying those words made her legs become unstable.

"And?" Jim placed his hands on her upper arms to hold her steady

"They swallow?" Her response was meek.

"That's correct." Maintaining his grip on her right arm to keep her upright, he moved in front of her, sat down on the couch, and then effortlessly eased her across his lap. "But I'm going to spank your bottom before I make you do that." He lifted her skirt and laid it across her back.

Jill murmured slightly as she felt Jim remove her panties and caress her naked behind. With her wrists fastened behind her back and lying across his lap as she was, she felt helpless. But once Jim began to spank her that helplessness made the spanking even more delicious. He was making her feel. Feel something she had no words for.

The spanking became harder and Jill's bottom became afire, prompting involuntary squirming and heavy panting. Suddenly her legs were pushed apart. Jim's right hand was rubbing her engorged clitoris. Her whole body shuddered, and as all muscle tension left her body she became limp on Jim's lap.

Jim, mercifully, caressed her hot bottom cheeks for the following several minutes while Jill slowly recovered from the orgasm. He then leaned over and whispered rhetorically into her ear, "I think we'd better put your onto your knees now, hadn't we."

Jim's hands on her arms, Jill was eased to her knees in front of the couch. He stood up, and she watched as he slowly unbuckled his belt, unzipped his pants, and released his ready cock. He pulled back the foreskin with his right hand and touched the glistening purple head to her barely parted lips. "Tongue," he ordered.

Jill opened her mouth and extended her tongue to lick the pre-cum from Jim's cock.

He then placed his left hand on the back of her head and pushed it forward until his cock was positioned in the middle of her still lapping tongue. "Now suck."

Jill closed her lips around the shaft and began rhythmic back and forth movements with her head while she sucked and continued to stimulate him with her tongue.

"I like having you as a good girl," Jim complemented her. "And I am going to cum in your mouth. But, first," he removed his cock and pushed her upper body down onto the couch, "I'm going to fuck you."

Jill's pussy was so soaked that his rigid cock effortlessly slid inside her. He held her hips, pulled back, and then slammed fully into her. Again and again, his abdomen slapped against her inflamed bottom cheeks while she had no option but to remain in place. Approaching orgasm, she pulled against the wrist restraints for a few seconds before screaming out as ecstasy flooded her body.

Jim withdrew and pulled Jill into a kneeling position on the floor. She stared at his solid erection before flitting her eyes upwards to his. "Wipe it first?" she asked sheepishly.

"No. I'm going to make you taste yourself too," he replied, then forced his throbbing cock between her lips. Almost ready to cum, Jim then grabbed Jill's head with both hands and proceeded to fuck her mouth. His hot ejaculate suddenly flooded across her tongue, but his hands kept her head in the position he wanted it. "Swallow and keep sucking," he ordered. "That's right."

After a few minutes, Jim released his grip and Jill's eyes looked up, searching for approval, as he withdrew his member from her mouth.

Jim put his pants back on, kissed the top of Jill's head, and untied her wrists. "I think you like being a good girl for me," he said as he helped her to her feet.

"You're right," she confessed. "Having you force me to do that was so hot, so erotic."

Jim started to open the bottle of mead he had brought while Jill pulled her panties back on and went into the kitchen for glasses and a platter of cheese and crackers. They sat cuddled up together on the couch. Jill's blouse was still unbuttoned, and she smiled when Jim slid her skirt up to where her panties were showing. Jill peered at him over the top of her wine glass. "You know, at first I wasn't sure," she told him. "But I think I might be submissive after all."

Jim returned her smile and topped up both of their glasses. "Here's to that realization," he said, clinking them together.

"I'd like to ask a big favor of you, Jim." Jill put her glass down on the table thoughtfully. "I have a sub who wants to be spanked hard, and you spank so much harder than I can."

"Are you talking about a man?"

"Yes. But he's very sub." She smiled. "Would you spank him for me?"

"No." Jim shook his head. "I don't think so."

"What about you being the schoolmaster?"

Jim looked quizzically at her.

"He also wants to be humiliated," she explained. "I can do that by having him dressed like a girl, in my schoolgirl uniform, so he'll look the part."

"You're saying that he's a sissy?"

"He isn't. At least, not yet." She smiled at Jim and tilted her head. "But he told me that it's a fantasy for him."

Jim looked directly back at her. "You do realize that this fantasy of his goes beyond a spanking, don't you?"

"What do you mean?"

"Humiliation. Being a sissy."

"But, but he's straight." Jill's hand went to her mouth for the moment of realization. "He's a happily married man with kids."

"In the 'real world' he is, yes." Jim grinned. "But we're talking about a fantasy world where he is a submissive. Apparently, there are more fantasies he wishes to explore, and he is looking to entrust you, his domme, to help him with them." He chuckled at Jill's confusion. "I'm confident that he is not gay or even curious in his regular life. But when one enters a submissive role, then gender goes out the window. It's all about sensuality. In this way a submissive can give him, or her, self over to pure feelings and experiences which cannot be a part of their everyday life."

"I see." Jill nodded. "That does make sense." She squirmed in her seat at her growing excitement that not only would Allan be spanked as a girl, but he would also be thanking Jim as one too. She twisted her mouth in an attempt to conceal a smirk. "Well?" She asked, leaning back on the couch. "Will you spank a sissy?" She smiled coyly. "I'll be there to thank you on his behalf, too."

Jim was thoughtful. "If I were to agree to something like that, I'd be wanting more than oral from you."

"Oh?' Jill pursed her lips, then reminded him, "I already told you that I won't do anal."

"I know." Jim grinned and nodded at her. "I have something else in mind. Something you'll find more sensual." He poured more mead. "Since you've realized you have a submissive side, I'd like to have you with a woman." He watched her eyes widen and added, "As a submissive, of course." Raising his right hand in anticipation of what she was about to say, he went on to explain. "Yes, I know you're not a lesbian, and I suspect you're not even curious. But, as I said earlier, we're not talking about your real world life."

Jill's internal reaction surprised her. Instead of an outright rejection of this suggestion, she realized that she was actually intrigued. If she would be willing to lick pussy, then she would be able to not only watch Allan be spanked, but also see him suck cock. That part was exciting, and in principal this deal seemed so equitable. Still, she needed time to process potentially being with a woman. Unsure and not ready to respond to Jim right away, she simply remained thoughtful, sipped her mead, and a thought occurred to her. She looked up. "Do you have a woman in mind that you want me to, um, be with?"

"I do. Her name is Lynn."

"Is Lynn the woman you said cums through anal?

"Yes, she is." Jim couldn't contain his grin, he liked where this was going.

"Would I be able to watch you do that to her?"

"Of course. Does this mean you want me to set it up?"

"Maybe," she twisted her mouth, more excited now but still unsure. "Can I take a day to think about it?"

"Of course," Jim responded. He, too, was dealing with potentially conflicting thoughts. He always enjoyed having a schoolgirl performing fellatio after he had administered a spanking, but had never considered the possibility of the 'schoolgirl' not being female. Was gender even relevant in the world of domination and submission, so long as all participants were consensual? Plus, since he was the dominant, why should it matter to him anyway?

More to the point for Jim was that having two submissive women together was an activity he wanted. Lynn, whom he had been dominating for some time, had recently told him she was becoming bi-curious, but being too hesitant to go out on her own, she had asked him, as her dominant, if he would facilitate. Jim had since become fascinated with the idea of having a threesome with her, and now that possibility looked to come to fruition.

Chapter Four: Sissy

Jill enjoyed converting Allan into a sissy schoolgirl. Prior to his arrival at her house she had instructed him to shave his legs, in addition to the requisite pubic hair removal that is generally required of submissives. She had obtained an old-style cheerleader outfit to dress him in. It had a pink and white striped, pleated skirt, and underneath she had him wear a pair of her white lace panties. She also fitted him with a wig of blonde, curly, shoulder length hair. After the final touches of knee socks and sneakers, along with a little rouge on Allan's cheeks, she stood back to admire her creation. Allan presented as a very convincing 'schoolgirl.' He even had nice legs.

When Jim arrived half an hour later, his reaction showed that he was also duly impressed.

They went into the living room and Jim sat on the couch while Jill, dressed in her schoolgirl uniform, and Allan stood side by side in front of him, holding hands. "This is Sissy," Jill told him. "Sissy has been very naughty and needs a good spanking."

"I see." Jim rubbed his chin. "Did you tell Sissy what I like to see?"

"No Sir, I forgot." She turned to Sissy. "Sir likes to have girls show him their panties."

"That's correct," Jim said. "So now I want both of you to lift up your skirts."

They both complied immediately.

"Matching panties are nice touch." Jim nodded his approval while admiring both Sissy's and Jill's legs. He then looked up. "Good choice, Jill."

"Thank you, Sir."

"Well Sissy. Are you ready for your spanking?" Jim asked, while taking Sissy's wrist in his left hand.

"Yes, Sir. I am."

"Splendid!" Jim pulled Sissy across his lap while Jill remained standing, excitedly watching, with her skirt still raised.

Jim flipped the cheerleader skirt up and began to rhythmically spank the revealed panties beneath. After two dozen strokes, he beckoned to Jill, "Pull Sissy's panties down. That's right. Take them all the way off. Good." He smiled over at her. "Now, remain kneeling right where you are."

Jim then commenced with a harder spanking across Sissy's already reddened buttocks. As the intensity increased, Sissy's panting combined with the audible slaps provided Jim with the familiar feelings he always achieved when giving a spanking. Spanking Sissy, it was turning out, was to be no different than with any other schoolgirl. However, instead of the normal manually bringing his victim to completion, he ordered Jill to do that.

Jill obediently wrapped Sissy's cock in the panties she was holding and slowly massaged it. With his hand on Sissy's neck to prevent movement, Jim delivered the final 6 spanks as it became obvious to all present that Sissy had been brought to climax.

After a short recovery time, Sissy slid info a kneeling position on the floor and Jim rose to his feet. Head down, Sissy asked,

"Please may I thank your for my spanking, Sir?" in a barely audible whisper.

"You may," Jim responded as he unfastened his belt.

While fellatio was expected, Jim was intrigued that his level of his arousal was so high. He eagerly produced his rigid rod and teasingly rubbed the glistening head against Sissy's partially parted lips. "I understand that this is your first time."

"Yes, Sir."

"Well, I am confident that you will do a good job for me. Open your mouth."

Sissy's mouth opened and sucked Jim's cock halfway in. Then, caressing it with his tongue, he began sliding his mouth up and down Jim's shaft.

Jim ejaculated after only a few minutes of sucking, and Sissy obligingly swallowed and kept sucking until, satisfied, Jim slid his cock out.

"Was I a good girl for you, Sir," Sissy asked.

"You were a very good girl, Sissy."

Jim pulled his clothing back together, and leaving Sissy still kneeling and staring at the floor he took Jill's hand and walked her into the hallway. "I'll be leaving now," He told her. "I want to hear feedback from you once you and your sub have had the chance to discuss today's scene." He grinned at her smiling face. "You liked watching that, didn't you?"

"Oh yes. I really did."

Jim smiled. "Not only are you submissive, but you're also a voyeur."

"I think I must be, yes." She smirked. "So, how was it for you?

"Sissy was good. I was surprised at how aroused I became. Are you looking forward to holding up your end of the deal?"

"I'll admit to being a bit nervous about it, but yes, I would say I am."

"Wonderful. Until Saturday, then. I'm looking forward to it." Jim brushed a stray lock of hair behind Jill's right ear. "And so is Lynn."

As soon as she closed the front door, Jill quickly took off her skirt. That was her submissive uniform, and right now she was anxious to go back to being a domme. Panties and blouse would suffice for that, along with the crop she had placed prior on the hallway table.

She returned to the living room where Allan was still kneeling on the floor. "You did well being a sissy cocksucker," she told him. "But now your mistress requires your service. Stand up and strip."

Allan immediately complied and stood naked with his hands behind his back.

"Bend over."

He forward with his hands on his knees and remained still while Jill gave him six swats with the crop on his behind. "Thank you mistress. Please may I service you now?"

Jill stood close in front of him and pushed his face into the front of her panties. "On your knees," she instructed. "And pull my panties down with your teeth."

Occasional cracks of the crop on his shoulders encouraged Allan to work quickly, and soon the panties floated down to Jill's ankles. She kicked them off and put her left hand on the back of Allan's head. "Lick me. Work your tongue," she told him as she grabbed his head and forced his mouth into her wet curls. Allan's tongue almost instantly provided the release that she needed.

Minutes later they sat together to drink wine and discuss Allan's first time being dominated by a man. "I loved it," he beamed. "Jim was perfect. Thank you so much for setting it up." He looked quizzical. "But I thought you said he only spanked women."

"That was correct," Jill smirked. "But I managed to convince him."

"How did you do that?"

"By doing what you just did."

Allan smiled. "Can you believe how erotic it is when he cums in your mouth."

"It was" she admitted. "Even more so when he made me swallow." Jill squirmed on her seat and shifted to look directly at Allan. "Jim says I might be a switch."

"Well, did you enjoy being in a submissive role?"

"Oh, yes. Very much so."

"Then you've answered your question."

"And you, Allan? Now that you've experienced it, would you want to be a sissy again?"

"Indeed." He drained his glass. "More even. I can't help but wonder what it would be like to go all the way with it."

Chapter Five: Lynn

Jill arrived at Jim's house shortly before two and nervously gripped the small bag she was carrying as she rang the doorbell. "Sorry if I'm a little early," she said as Jim opened the door.

"Not at all, come on in," he said warmly. "Why don't you get comfortable and we'll have some refreshment. There is a bathroom just down the hall."

Lynn arrived while Jill was getting changed. Before Jim opened the door she unfastened the front of her long raincoat so reveal the short schoolgirl outfit beneath, and as she entered Jim helped her out of the coat and hung it in the hallway closet. "Jill will be right with us," he told her. "Let's go into the living room."

The coffee table was set with a bottle of mead and 3 glasses. Lynn sat at one end of the couch and Jim opened the wine as Jill entered the room. "Come on in, Jill," he beckoned. "I'd like you to meet Lynn."

Lynn smiled and quickly stood up. "Hello, Jill." She gave Jill a kiss on the cheek and embraced her. "I like your uniform."

"It's a pleasure to meet you, too, Lynn." Jill responded, her earlier trepidation suddenly having left her due to Lynn's friendly greeting. "I think your skirt is shorter than mine."

Jim poured the mead, gave each of the women a glass, and the three of them then sat together on the couch with Jill in the middle.

"I'll tell you a secret," Lynn whispered to Jill. "Since my skirt is so short I'm not allowed to wear any panties with it because they would show from behind."

After a few minutes of friendly small talk, their glasses drained, Jim told Jill to put her arms across the back of the couch. Her left arm behind him, he placed his right arm around her, holding her right arm in place. He then nuzzled into the left side of her neck while his free hand began to fondle her breasts through her thin cotton blouse. He then toyed with top button and whispered, "Lynn is going to help me unbutton your blouse," into her ear.

Lynn turned towards them and her right hand joined in with Jim as they slowly unfastened the front of Jill's blouse. The final button undone, Jim took Lynn's hand and moved it to Jill's right breast, uncovering it in the process.

Lynn leaned forward and, tentatively at first, licked each of Jill's nipples. She then looked up. Jill's eyes were partially closed and deep breaths were coming from between her parted lips, encouraging Lynn to massage the naked breasts before her while sucking the nipples to arousal.

Jim stroked Lynn's hair, then nibbled on Jill's left ear. "I think it's time to let Lynn look up your skirt," he told her, then stood up and eased her to her feet. He positioned Jill in front of Lynn, who remained sitting on the couch, and stood behind her, holding her. He then slid his hands down her sides to the hem of her skirt and slowly raised it up, holding it at waist level. Jill laid her head back on his left shoulder and Lynn excitedly reached out to stroke the front of the exposed panties. She looked up a Jim. "May I pull them down, Sir?" she asked.

"I want you to take them completely off," he replied, clutching Jill tighter as she began to tremble.

Panties soon gone, Jim laid Jill on the couch with her head on the armrest, her right leg extended on the couch and her left foot on the floor. Lynn knelt next to Jill's spread legs and, at Jim's encouragement, leaned forward and extended her tongue. She began to lick.

Jim watched until Jill began to pant and buck, then knelt to caress her breasts and watched her face as Lynn delivered her into orgasm. She was still in an almost entranced state when Jim moved her into a sitting position and she eagerly returned the affection when Lynn sat next to her and kissed her. When they slowly parted, Jim took both of their hands in his and pulled them to their feet. "We're going upstairs now," he told them.

Jim directed them into the guest bedroom and Lynn sat on the edge of the bed with her legs apart. Jim stood behind Jill as she stared at the shaved mound now visible under Lynn's short skirt. "It's time to say thank you to Lynn, now," he told her, then eased her to her knees.

Lynn slid her skirt up past her waist as Jill mouth approached her pussy, then laid back as Jill's tongue made contact.

"That's a good girl," Jim encouraged Jill as her licking became bolder. He then told Lynn to spread her legs wide with her hands behind her knees, opening her slit for Jill's now probing tongue.

While Jill continued cunnilingus, Jim quickly undressed. He then eased Jill's head back and ordered her to suck his erect cock. She took it all the way in, but after only a few seconds he pulled it out and teased Lynn's quivering pussy with the bulbous head.

"Fuck me, please," Lynn panted. "Fuck me and lick me."

Jim thrust into her, then pushed Jill's head down. "Lick her clit," he ordered as he began to rhythmically fuck Lynn. It took mere seconds before Lynn arched her back and gasped in the throes of delight.

Jim withdrew his cock and Jill took it in her mouth and sucked without hesitation. He stopped her before completion, though. It was the next activity where that was to occur.

"Now, Jill. You are to strip Lynn."

Jill eagerly began to unbutton Lynn's blouse, fondling and licking her breasts once she had the garment off, then quickly removed her skirt. While this was happening, Jim opened a dresser drawer, took out four leather restraints with silver buckles and loops with carabiner clips, and attached them to Lynn's wrists and ankles. "Hands and knees," he instructed.

Lynn compliantly turned over, positioned herself on her hands and knees in the center of the bed, then put her head down and reached her hands back towards her ankles. Jim then clipped her ankles and wrists together and pushed her knees apart. Jill sat on the bed staring at how Lynn was now immobilized, her head lying sideways on the bed and her bottom up and fully exposed.

Jim then produced a small, leather whip and a tube of lubricant. He began to flog Lynn's bottom until red streaks appeared, then directed his strokes to her parted labia lips. When fully reddened, he put the instrument down and squeezed some lotion onto the tip of his right forefinger. "This both soothes," he said as he applied it to her engorged clitoris, "And excites.

Lynn began to moan and it was clear that she was straining against the restraints, but to no avail. Applying more lube to his finger, Jim then inserted two fingers into her twitching vagina, eliciting a gasp. He pushed them in and out and then turned them so that they were lying against her g-spot, while his thumb was on top of her clit. He squeezed them together, and with a few fast movements drove Lynn into another orgasm.

"Women are naturally multi-orgasmic," he explained to a very attentive Jill. "So at this point I can make her cum as often as I want.

Fingers still inside Lynn's vagina, Jim turned his hand sideways and inserted a third, then a fourth finger, while positioning his thumb over her puckered anal entrance. He pushed his whole hand in, four fingers into her pussy and thumb up her backside, slid them almost out, then moved one finger next to his thumb and re-inserted.

Lynn moaned with uncontrollable delight as Jim continued to excite her.

"What should I do with you now?" He asked.

"Please, Sir," she murmured. "Please fuck my ass."

Jim slid his hands away and positioned his cock, just pushing the bulb into her at first. He then leaned towards her, forcing it slowly inside. He grabbed her hips, slid out half way, then slowly pushed back in. "This get her nicely warmed up," he told Jill. "So she is ready to be fucked like this her properly."

"Please may I cum, Sir," Lynn pleaded as Jim thrust back and forth into her bottom.

"Not until I do," he replied.

"Please, Sir," she begged. "Please cum up my ass. Please."

Jim pounded into her faster and faster, his abdomen smacking against her buttocks with each thrust, until he said, "You can cum now," and then froze with his cock buried deep inside her. He remained that way while Lynn's pulsing anal muscles continued to milk his member. Once they subsided, he unclipped the restraints and Lynn slid forward into a face-down position on the bed as Jim withdrew from her.

He lay down next to her and instructed Jill to lie on the other side, each of them holding her until, a few minutes later, she turned over and smiled at them both. "It takes me a bit to recover after that," she explained. "But I love it. The feeling is indescribable."

"I've never been butt fucked," Jill admitted, while her left hand wandered over Lynn' breasts. "Do you cum that hard every time?"

Lynn turned to Jill and kissed her. "Every time," she confirmed. "You should try it."

Chapter Six: Two Threesomes

Unexpectedly, Jill had thoroughly enjoyed being with a woman, kissing her, licking her pussy and being licked. So long as she was in the submissive role she had no problem with doing as she was told. However, it was the image of Lynn being tied up and butt fucked that remained in the forefront of her mind that night. It had been so exciting to watch Lynn achieve such obvious pleasure, and it caused Jill to wonder how it might feel to have that done to her. Today had certainly opened her eyes to the possibilities available to her as a sub.

In her role as a domme, she couldn't help but think about how arousing it would be to order Allan to have his ass fucked by Jim. She had realized that was what Allan must have meant when he said he wanted to go all the way as a sissy. She smiled, knowing that Jim would likely consent to doing so if she would let him have her that way too.

Jill enjoyed vivid dreams that night.

Having had a few days to process their activities, Jim and Jill met for lunch the following Wednesday to discuss. Jill reported that Allan was thrilled with becoming Sissy. The hard spanking was just what he wanted, and being humiliated into performing fellatio afterwards was exciting for him. She smiled at Jim. "Allan said to tell you that he would like more."

"Lynn was delighted with being with you, too. Her curiosity has confirmed to her that she is definitely a bisexual sub. So," Jim took a quaff of coffee, "You and I should discuss whether these sessions were just one-offs, or are they something that we would like to continue with."

"How do you feel about that?"

"I've given it some thought," he put his coffee cup down. "And if you would like me to continue to spank Sissy I will agree, provided that you participate in threesomes with Lynn and myself."

"What exactly would these threesomes entail?"

"You would join Lynn in being completely submissive to me. In addition to my alternating attention between the two of you, you would also do things with each other as I direct." He smiled. "Basically, both of you will be bisexual subs when you're with me."

"I see." Jill took a drink of water and twisted her mouth. "And would you go further with Allan if I agreed to that?"

"What are you thinking?"

"He told me he wants to go all the way as a sissy." She leaned across the table and whispered, "So I want to watch you fuck him up the ass." She sat upright again. "As his domme, I will order him to submit to you for that. If you agree, then I'll do threesomes with you and Lynn."

"Hmm," Jim rubbed his chin and a glint appeared in his eye as he looked back at her across the table.

"I'll be fine with that too," she said. It was clear that Jill understood what Jim had in mind. Actually, this was the deal she wanted. "If you'll fuck Sissy, then I'll let you fuck me up my ass. But only when I'm submissive." She raised her right index finger.

"And when we're playing with Allan, I'm always going to be his domme."

JILL'S FRONT DOOR OPENED after Jim rang the bell, and as he expected she was hiding behind it. We wasn't expecting to see her in her domme leathers after he entered, however. "Very sexy," he said, while he stared at her legs.

Then entered the living room where Sissy was standing attentively in the center of the rug. In addition to the cheerleader uniform, Sissy was also waring a leather collar. Jill hooked her right index finger through the silver metal loop in front and led Sissy behind the couch. "Lean over," she instructed as she pulled her finger away.

Jim stood next to her.

"As you can see, Jim," she said as she raised the skirt and laid it across Sissy's back, revealing a pre-reddened, naked bottom. "Sissy has been prepared for you to right away spank hard."

Jim smiled, nodded to Jill, and proceeded to deliver a series of twenty hard slaps, alternating between Sissy's now glowing buttock cheeks.

Jill once again grabbed the collar and stood a quivering Sissy upright and walked him back to the center of the carpet. "Get on your knees. Now, what do you say?"

"Please may I thank you for my spanking, Sir."

"You may," Jim answered while removing his pants. "Take it deep."

Sissy sucked Jim's cock nearly all the way in, then continued to slide his mouth back and forth until Jill told him to stop. "Lean forward on your hands and knees," she instructed. "Jim is now going to fuck you." She swatted his bottom with her crop. "And you're going to keep still while he does."

"Yes, mistress."

Jill then produced a tube of lubricant and generously applied it to Sissy's bottom hole. First inserting one finger, then two, before moving them around. She pulled her fingers away and looked up at Jim. 'Sissy is all ready for you now."

Jim knelt behind Sissy and positioned the head of his cock against the puckered entrance. He had previously wondered if he would be able to go through with this. Although Sissy presented as a convincing girl, Jim was still aware that Sissy was a man and, knowing this, had been concerned that he might not achieve sufficient hardness. He was, however, very rigid from the sucking. He entered Sissy easily, in spite of some sphincter resistance. Half way inside and holding onto Sissy's hips, he pulled back slightly and then slid nearly all the way in.

Jill, intently watching so far, then pulled up her skirt and positioned herself on the floor, legs spread on either side of Sissy's head. "Service me while you're being fucked," she ordered. "Do a good job and I'll let you touch yourself."

Jill came first, grabbing Sissy's head in she succumbed to waves of delight. She then let go and told Sissy to masturbate. He squirted into his hand as soon as he touched his unbelievably hard cock, and the resultant waves of muscle activity quickly caused Jim to ejaculate deep inside him.

Allan had become a proper sissy.

A week later, Jim had Jill and Lynn back at his house. Dressed in their schoolgirl outfits, he had them kneeling side by side between his spread legs, each taking turns sucking his cock while the other licked and sucked his scrotum. It was a wonderful sensation, and he held out as long as was possible. Eventually, however, he succumbed to ejaculating in Lynn's mouth, who then forced her tongue into Jill's mouth. "Equal shares," she cooed as their lips finally parted, each having swallowed their portion of cum.

"Good girls," Jim told them as he kissed each of them on the top of her head. He leaned back on the couch and told them to stand up. "Now, strip each other while kissing and caressing."

Jim felt his cock becoming restored as he watched the show they were putting on for him. Once they were both naked, they stood in front of him holding hands, awaiting his next instruction.

"We're going to the bedroom now," he told them. It was delightful walking behind them as they ascended the stairs, fondling their buttocks as they moved. He told Jill to lie on the bed, then instructed Lynn to ease her pussy over Jill's mouth and massage her breasts. Lynn rocked back and forth, forcing Jill's tongue into the furrow between her labia lips, until Jim pushed her head down between Jill's legs. "You're now going to lick each other," he told them. "Try to make the other cum."

As the women engaged in this 69 position in glorious abandon, Jim stripped and positioned himself behind Lynn. His cock slid into her soaked pussy with ease, and Jill extended her licking to include his balls as he fucked Lynn from behind. She came within minutes, so Jim withdrew and told her to roll off Jill.

Jill, almost at the point of cumming, watched excitedly as Jim fastened the restraints onto ankles, then ordered her to roll over onto her hands and knees. Her ankles were then clipped to ties on either side of the bed, causing her to rest on her lower arms while her bottom was up in the air, legs firmly fixed apart. She gasped when she felt the cool lubricant being applied to her bottom and Jim's finger teased her anal opening. He worked slowly inserting two fingers when she had loosened up, but her sphincter kept involuntarily squeezing down on them.

Lynn laid down next to her, looking up into her face, then pulled her into a tongue sharing kiss. Slowly parting, she smiled. "Relax, Jill," she said. "Jim is going make you feel so good."

While Lynn was distracting Jill, Jim had removed his fingers and already had his purple bulb up against Jill's puckered entrance. He applied just enough pressure so that each time her sphincter relaxed his cock eased in a little further. Once halfway in, however, he tightened his grip on the hips and began to slide in and out. A bit further with each stroke.

Jill attempted to move forward as he entered her, but was unable to move.

"What's happening, Jill?" Lynn asked her, while sliding her hand underneath and rubbing Jill's clitoris.

"I'm being fucked up my ass." Jill could barely get the words out, but doing so added to her arousal.

Jim at this time had begun a steady in and out. Jill's ass had relaxed to take him in, and she was clearly starting to enjoy it as she gasped into orgasm.

Moving in front of her, Lynn spread her legs, and pushed Jill's mouth down onto her soaked pussy. Each thrust Jim made into her ass pushed her tongue inside. Another orgasm flooded her, then another. Jill suddenly felt she was in an otherworldly place. Her whole body was flooded with waves of sensations and all she knew was that she felt both strange and wonderful.

After a long five minutes Jill came around and realized that she was lying between Jim and Lynn, being caressed by them both. "Was I in subspace?" She asked, still feeling a little disoriented.

"Indeed!' Lynn replied. "You're a lucky girl."

ONE DAY, MONTHS LATER, Jim found himself musing contemplatively about the adventures he had enjoyed since meeting Jill. Lynn was his primary submissive, but Jill had added a wonderful dimension to his dominating her. She frequently joined in with him and Lynn for some truly arousing threesomes.

In exchange, Jim occasionally went to Jill's house where, together, they dominated her submissive, Allan, who became Sissy when Jim joined their play. This was pure role play submission for Allan. He wanted to dress and be treated like a girl, and he did a good job of it too. For threesomes at Jill's house, Sissy was just as much a girl as Jill as far as Jim was concerned.

But it was Jill who felt she benefited the most from this arrangement. She had not only uncovered, but had thoroughly immersed herself in her submissive side, without affecting her role as a domme. She had also realized that she was a voyeur, and by engaging in both threesome scenarios she had the opportunity to indulge in that. Finally, she had come to understand that sexual orientation and gender is irrelevant to a submissive. D/s play is all about feeling and sensuality. No matter what they did in their special times together, in the real world, she, Allan, and Lynn would remain perfectly straight.

THE END